## Stories and rhymes in this book

HELLO FROM THE HIPPOS

HILDA'S HAT

ENTERTAINING HIPPOS

SURPRISE!

A HEALTHY HIPPO

A L-O-N-G WALK

ARE HIPPOS HORRIBLE?

HORRIBLE CREEPY CRAWLIES!

HAPPINESS

Published by Ladybird Books Ltd
27 Wrights Lane London W8 5TZ
A Penguin Company
3 5 7 9 10 8 6 4 2

© LADYBIRD BOOKS LTD MCMXCIX

Produced for Ladybird Books Ltd by Nicola Baxter and Amanda Hawkes
The moral rights of the autor/illustrator have been asserted
LADYBIRD and the device of a Ladybird are trasmitted of Ladybird Books Ltd

Printed in Italy

# The Horrible Hippos

by Nicola Baxter

illustrated by Julie Buchanan-Black

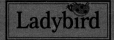

# HELLO FROM THE HIPPOS

We're the Horrible Hippos
And we're happy
When we're munching,

But socks,                     and clocks,

and
hollyhocks,

Take quite a bit
of crunching!

Mum Hilda tries to keep
things nice,

But Hilary
chews them
in a trice.

And Hilary is only two...
Look what Great Aunt
Hortense can do!

If Horrible Hippos
you should meet,
Make sure they've
all had lots to eat!

# HILDA'S HAT

Hilda Hippo had a brand new hat. She thought it was GORGEOUS!

She put it safely in a box...

away from other Horrible Hippos.

One morning, Hilda set off
early with Hilary to do
some shopping.

Great Aunt Hortense was
still in bed.

When her alarm clock rang...

she ate it!

Then she jumped out of bed and did her morning exercises...

bending...

and s-t-r-e-t-c-h-i-n-g.

"Now I'm
REALLY
hungry,"
she said,
marching
downstairs.

Great Aunt Hortense enjoyed her usual breakfast...

a triple-decker sponge cake,

a fat, frilly, flowered cushion,

a jar of
pickled
onions,

half a
handbag

and three banana
milkshakes.
But still she felt peckish.

She wanted just one mouthful of something really tasty...

Much, much later, Hilda and Hilary came home with their shopping.

"My feet are killing me!" said Hilda, limping upstairs to give them a soak.

Suddenly, there came a HORRIBLE yell!

"It was
delicious!"
said
Hortense.

"It IS
delicious!"
said Hilary.

"Well, I AM rather hungry,"
sighed Hilda. "Pass me that
hat, Hortense. Mmmmmm!"

# ENTERTAINING HIPPOS

If a hippo comes to supper,
Hide your comics
and your toys,

And tell your
favourite
teddy bear

Not to make
a noise.

"We've brought you breakfast in bed," said Hilary.

"Don't eat the tray, dear," said Great Aunt Hortense.

# "GO AWAY!"

cried poor Hilda. "It's half past five in the morning!"

"Ooops!" The two Horrible Hippos crept loudly away.

"This is a really HORRIBLE day!" groaned Hilda.

When Hilda woke up later, she put on her best dress. But... it was too small!

"This is a really HORRIBLE day!" she said, pulling on her old dress.

But down in the sitting room, Hilda had a big surprise.

The Horrible Hippos were waiting with presents and a cake and a special song...

Hippo birthday to you!
Hippo birthday to you!
Hippo birthday, dear hippo,
Hippo birthday to YOOUUU!

"This is a really
WONDERFUL day!" smiled
Hilda Horrible Hippo.

# A HEALTHY HIPPO

When a hippo has
A tummy ache
And feels distinctly sick,
She can take a pill
And still feel ill...

But a doctor does the trick!

# A L-O-N-G WALK

Zippo Hippo had come to
visit Hilda.

"Would you come for a
walk with me on Saturday?"
he asked.

"We'd love to come," said Great Aunt Hortense.

"Oh... hmm," said Zippo.

On Saturday, the three Horrible Hippos got ready. They took a little snack.

The Horrible Hippos met
Zippo in the woods.
"This way!" he called.

They walked for miles...

and miles...

and miles.

"This is FUN!" cried Zippo.

"This is AWFUL!" moaned Hilda and Hilary and Great Aunt Hortense.

# ARE HIPPOS HORRIBLE?

We're not horribly horrid,

We're not horribly rough,

We're just horribly hungry,
We can't eat enough!

# HORRIBLE CREEPY CRAWLIES!

One day Hilda went to the cupboard and found it was bare.

"We should grow our own fruit and vegetables," she said.

"We could munch strawberries all day long."

"We could crunch carrots and cabbages," said Great Aunt Hortense.

"And creepy caterpillars!"

muttered
Great Aunt
Hortense.

"And slugs!"

said Hilda.

# HAPPINESS

A rumbly
tummy makes
hippos sad,

They get
shortish and
sharpish and
snappy.

A fabulous feed is what
they need...

To be
Horrible
Hippo
happy!